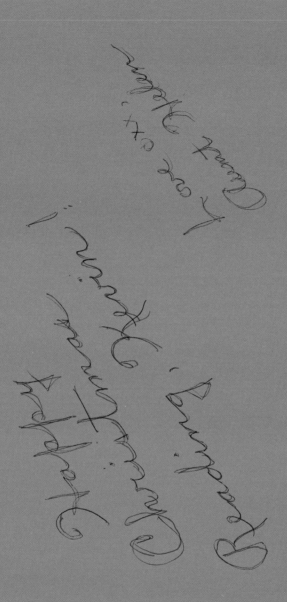

LEONARD B. LUBIN

CHRISTMAS GIFT-BRINGERS

Lothrop, Lee & Shepard Books
New York

First Edition   1 2 3 4 5 6 7 8 9 10

Library of Congress Cataloging in Publication Data

Lubin, Leonard B. Christmas gift-bringers/Leonard B. Lubin.
p.   cm.
Summary: Stories of the traditional bringers of Christmas gifts around the world persuade a skeptical youngster to believe in Santa Claus.
ISBN 0-688-07019-1.—ISBN 0-688-07020-5 (lib. bdg.)   1. Christmas—Juvenile literature. [1. Christmas. 2. Santa Claus.]   I. Title.   GT4985.5.L83   1989   391.2'68282—dc19
89-2292   CIP   AC

For
All My Friends
with
much love, care, and affection
"God Bless Us Every One"
Merry Christmas
L.B.L.

I

t was Christmas Eve. In their attic home, the mouse family prepared for the arrival of Santa Claus.

"I will put out a plate of cookies and a glass of milk for Santa!" Sara announced importantly.

"Santa's coming! Santa's coming!" baby Ben chimed in.

"Santa, Santa, Santa! Phooey! I say there is no Santa. Never was. Never will be!" declared Sidney.

"Why, Sidney! What a thing to say!" Father mouse admonished. He set aside his evening paper and gave his eldest son a stern look.

"No Santa?" Sara and Ben asked at the same moment.

"Sidney, if I were you, I wouldn't be so sure of myself. Santa Claus has been important to a lot of people for a long time."

"Yea, Santa!" cheered Ben.

"HUMPH!" grunted Sidney.

"I see Sidney needs to be convinced," Father said. "All of you follow me to the other side of the attic. I know just the thing to clear up Sidney's doubts. Now stay close and don't dawdle."

"Yea, Santa!" Ben piped up again.

They each lit a candle and, with Father in the lead, ventured across the moonlit attic. Among cardboard cartons, up and over mountains of crockery and yellowed newspapers, under an old baby carriage, and past a wide-eyed doll in a pink dress they scampered hurriedly. Sara couldn't resist stopping to ooh and aah over the doll, but she quickly caught up with the rest of the family.

When they came to a pile of old books, Father mouse led them up the stack. After they had caught their breath, Father said, "Here we are. This, Sidney," pointing to an old-fashioned picture book, "will show you that Santa has been around a long, long time, in many different places in the world. Let's see what we can find out about him."

With that, Father opened the book and began the story of the Christmas gift-bringers.

Saint Nicholas

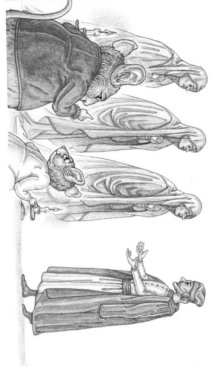

Saint Nicholas was a humble, kind, and generous man who lived many centuries ago in a part of the world now called Turkey. Many legends tell of his good and thoughtful deeds. When he died, almost seventeen hundred years ago, he was so well liked that people began to call him a saint.

One story about him explains how he became known as a gift-bringer. When he was a very young man, Nicholas heard of a poor merchant who was about to sell his three daughters into slavery because he didn't have money to provide them with dowries. In those days no one would marry a woman without a dowry. The merchant was a good man who loved his daughters, and if he couldn't find husbands for them, he hoped he could find a slave-master who would be kind to them. Nicholas was touched by the poor man's difficult decision. One night he went to the merchant's house and tossed three bags of gold, one for each of the daughters, in through an open window. It is said that the bags of gold landed in the girls' stockings, which were hung to dry before the fireplace. The gold

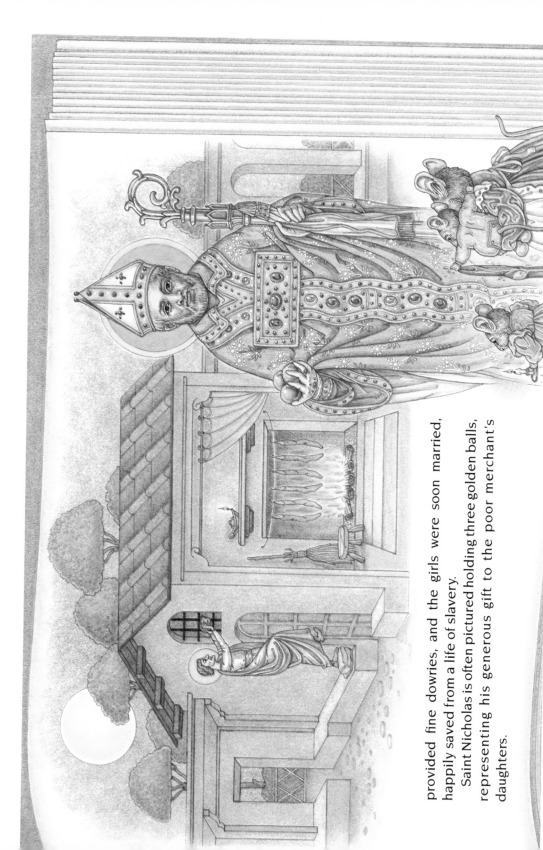

provided fine dowries, and the girls were soon married, happily saved from a life of slavery.

Saint Nicholas is often pictured holding three golden balls, representing his generous gift to the poor merchant's daughters.

Sinter Claes and Black Peter

When people in other countries heard about Saint Nicholas and the three bags of gold, they adopted him as their gift-bringer. The Eve of Saint Nicholas (December 5, his birthday) became the time to give gifts.

In Holland Sinter Claes arrives late at night. Dressed in his bishop's robes, he rides through the quiet streets on a white horse, accompanied by his servant Black Peter. Black Peter, a fearsome creature, has a soot-covered face, fiery red eyes, and horns on his head. He carries a huge

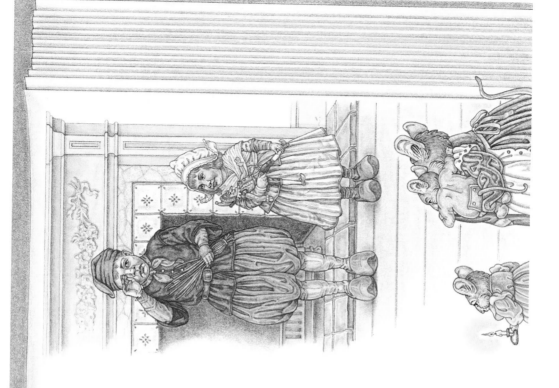

sack filled with presents for the good children and birch rods for the bad. It is he, at the saint's bidding, who climbs down the chimney and leaves gifts in wooden shoes that children have placed by the hearth.

When the Dutch came to the New World, they brought Sinter Claes with them. Eventually the celebration of gift-giving became mingled with the Christmas holiday, and Santa Claus, as he became known, then arrived on Christmas Eve.

Father Christmas

Raise up high your cup of cheer,
For Father Christmas, at last, is here!

When the Romans occupied England almost two thousand years ago, they brought with them the celebration of Saturnalia, in honor of the god Saturn, who was in charge of winter festivities. The English continued to celebrate the winter holiday after the Romans left, but they adapted it to suit themselves. The central figure who presided over the merrymaking eventually became known as Father Christmas.

Father Christmas, a bearded giant of a man, is dressed in a fur-trimmed scarlet robe and crowned with a wreath of holly. He is a symbol of eating, drinking, and other

holiday traditions, and is a gift-bringer as well. The appearance of Father Christmas during the Christmas season (especially on Boxing Day, December 26, when the churches open their alms boxes and give to the poor), inspires joy, peace on earth, and good will to all. Other holiday symbols associated with Father Christmas in "Merrie Old England" are the boar's head, the wassail bowl, and the flaming plum pudding, without which no English Christmas dinner would be complete!

The history of French Christmas traditions is very much like that of the English. In France, Father Christmas is known as Père Noël.

Christkindl

The Christkindl (the name means "Christ Child") brings gifts to German and Austrian households, as well as to Pennsylvania Dutch families living in the United States. An angelic childlike figure with golden wings, the Christkindl is dressed in a flowing white robe and wears a jeweled crown. A door or window is left ajar on Christmas Eve, and the Christkindl enters with the sound of tinkling bells. After helping decorate the family *Tannenbaum* (Christmas tree), the Christkindl distributes cookies, candies, toys, and small bundles containing knitted mittens, caps, and scarves. Occasionally a birch rod is tied to a bundle to remind a naughty child to be on better behavior in the New Year. When Germans emigrated to America, *Christkindl* was translated into English as "Kriss Kringle," which eventually became thought of (quite wrongly) as another name for Santa Claus.

In France the Christkindl is known as Le Petit Noël and often accompanies Père Noël on his holiday travels. Le Petit Noël symbolizes the religious side of the Christmas holiday, and Père Noël represents its festive aspects.

Jultomten and Julbock

The Jultomten is the Swedish Christmas elf. He lives in the hayloft or attic and guards the household during the year. Very small in size and sporting a red woolen cap and a long white beard, the Jultomten rides through the countryside on Christmas Eve in a sleigh pulled by the Julbock (Yule goat). The Julbock is made entirely of straw and is one of Sweden's favorite Christmas symbols. As this jolly pair make their rounds of gift-giving, they discover an offering of rice pudding on the doorstep of each house, left there by the family to ensure the Jultomten's protection in the coming year.

Julnisse

The Julnisse is the Jultomten's Danish relative. He also is an attic-dwelling elf who protects the household. The Julnisse is a mischievous character, however, and often "misplaces" household items as a way of making his presence known. He is fond of animals, and can be seen only by the family cat.

Star Man

In Poland the star is the most popular Christmas symbol. The holiday festivities begin when the first star appears in the sky on Christmas Eve. After putting the decorations on their Christmas tree, many of which are star-shaped, the family have a traditional Christmas Eve supper, which for good luck must have an odd number of dishes and an even number of diners! The children then eagerly await the arrival of the Star Man.

The children's gifts are said to come from the stars, and the Star Man, usually the village priest, is the holiday gift-bringer. He is accompanied by the Star Boys, a band of children dressed in fanciful costumes to repre-

sent the Wise Men and Shepherds of the Nativity. The Star Man and Star Boys carry a star-shaped paper lantern and go from house to house singing Christmas carols. At each household the Star Man quizzes the children in their religious instruction and rewards them with small gifts, fruit, and candies. In turn, the Star Boys are given treats in payment for their caroling.

Saint Nicholas appears bearing gifts to Polish children on January 6, the day the Wise Men are said to have arrived in Bethlehem to see the Christ Child, so children in Poland receive presents from two different gift-bringers during the Christmas season.

The Magi

The Magi are among the best-known Christmas gift-bringers. They are said to have come from the Orient (the East), following a bright star that led them to the stable in Bethlehem where the baby Jesus lay in a manger. *Magi* means "Wise Men." How many Magi there were originally, and exactly where they came from, remains a mystery. Through the centuries, tradition fixed their number at three, and they became known as kings. They were given names, and each is said to be of a particular race, age, and country.

Melchior is the oldest, with a full white beard. He was king of Arabia, and brought a casket of gold as a gift to the Christ Child. Balthasar was king of Ethiopia, about forty years old, and

Black. He brought a gift of myrrh, a soothing healing ointment. Caspar, a young man of twenty, was king of Tarsus, and his gift was a jar of fragrant frankincense. Their journey came to an end on January 6, Epiphany or Three Kings' Day. In Spain, Mexico, and other Spanish-speaking countries, the Three Kings bring children holiday gifts on Epiphany. On the evening before, children put out straw, grain, and water for the camels the Wise Men are said to have ridden. The next morning, the straw, grain, and water have disappeared, and gifts are left in their place.

The Magi represent people of all races and ages, and are symbols of reverence, loving, and giving.

Befana ✳ Babouschka

Italy and Russia, though separated by great distance, have similar legends about the Christmas gift-bringer. In Italy a witchlike, wrinkled old lady known as Befana was busy cleaning her house when the Three Kings stopped to ask if she would accompany them in their search for the Christ Child. She refused, claiming she had too much to do, and the Wise Men went on their way.

In Russia an equally old and wrinkled crone named Babouschka not only refused to go with the Wise Men, but pointed them in the wrong direction as well! Both Befana and Babouschka had second thoughts, and the next day decided to try to catch up with the Wise Men. They

both are said still to be on their quest for the Christ Child.

On Epiphany Eve, Befana and Babouschka wander through the towns and countryside, entering the houses of rich and poor alike. They peer into cradles and beds at sleeping infants and children, always with the question, "Is this the one?" They leave a small gift behind and continue their search.

After the story of Befana and Babouschka, Father closed the book and said, "Well, Sidney, what do you think about Santa Claus now?" The mouse family turned to look at Sidney ...but Sidney was gone!

The mice hurried back home as fast as they could, and were relieved to find Sidney hanging up his stocking on the chimney.

He smiled sheepishly and said with conviction, "Yea, Santa!"

"Yea, Santa!" Mother, Father, and Sara exclaimed with delight.

"Yea, Sidney!" baby Ben cheered happily.

For Further Reading

Barth, Edna. *Holly, Reindeer and Colored Lights.* Clarion Books, 1971.

Del Re, Gerard & Patricia. *The Christmas Almanack.* Doubleday & Company, Inc., 1979.

Giblin, James Cross. *The Truth About Santa Claus.* Thomas Y. Crowell, 1985.

Kuse, James, editorial director. *The Ideals Christmas Treasury.* Ideals Publishing Corp., 1978.

The Life Book of Christmas. Vol. I, *The Glory of Christmas.* Vol. II, *The Pageantry of Christmas.* Vol. III, *The Merriment of Christmas.* Time, Inc., 1963.

Miles, Clement A. *Christmas Customs and Traditions.* Dover Publications, Inc., 1976.

Parents' Magazine Press. Parents' Magazine Christmas Holiday Book. Parents' Magazine Enterprises, Inc., 1972.